AN

Illustrated by Kate Aldous

Hutchinson
London Melbourne Auckland Johannesburg

ill it be fine?" murmured Laura to herself, gazing up at the pale blue sky. "Oh *please* let it be fine!"

She was standing in the back garden of the end house, where she lived with her parents and her younger brother Edmund, in the village of Lark Rise.

After a moment she pulled herself up and perched on the wall of the pig sty to talk to the Dinner Pig.

"It simply *has* to be sunny tomorrow," she said.

The Dinner Pig had no opinion on the weather, being busily and noisily

engaged with a pan of potato peelings.
But for Laura it was terribly important.

For tomorrow was May Day, the most
exciting day of the whole year for the
children of Lark Rise. The day they
carried the May garland round the village
in procession, with the Lady in all her
finery, and the May Queen in her crown.

Today, the last day of April, school would start extra early and the children would spend all day dressing the garland, while the May Queen made her crown from glossy leaves and big garden daisies.

Laura went out of the gate at the end of the garden, and began picking flowers along the side of the new green corn in the field: buttercups and cow parsley and daisies and violets and primroses. She thought about her best friend, Ella May Sowerby, who was to be May Queen.

"You choose me this year," Ella May had whispered in class, giving Laura's arm a friendly squeeze that felt more like a pinch, "and I'll choose you next year."

Ella May was a big girl and Laura wanted to stay friends with her. The result was, Ella May had been behaving like a queen for the past three weeks, which had been very annoying.

All the same, nothing could spoil Laura's excitement. When she went back into the house with her arms full of flowers, there was her mother bustling about getting breakfast, but no sign of Edmund. "Laura, there you are," said her mother. "Run upstairs will you, and hurry that brother of yours. He'd stay asleep if the house was falling down!" And she smiled, not a bit cross, to think of Edmund snoring while the house collapsed.

When they at last left for school, Laura and Edmund were loaded down with flowers and greenery and long grasses, so that they looked more like walking bushes than two perfectly ordinary children. And all along the road were other children, much more eager to get to school than usual, staggering

beneath their offerings for the
garland.

In the schoolroom Miss Ho
the children to work at once. The big
garland, four feet high, had to be dressed
all over in posies, so that not a scrap of
wood or wire could be seen, and
crowned with flowers of yellow and gold.

In a special corner behind Miss Holmes's desk, Ella May worked on her crown. Once, Laura went over to watch her.

"Would you like some help, Ella May?" she asked politely, itching to have a go.

"No thank you, Laura," replied Ella May, very haughty and distant. "This is my job, you know."

"Come along Laura," called Miss Holmes, "and let Ella May finish her work!"

Laura blushed a fiery red. But Edmund left the other boys just for a moment, and said gruffly to her: "Don't mind old Ella May. She's not half as pretty as she thinks she is." At last the garland was ready. And now came the great moment when the Lady was to be taken out.

The Lady was a beautiful doll in a blue silk dress, who lived from one May Day to the next at the bottom of Miss Holmes's big sewing box. She was even more important than the May Queen, for she was to be fixed to the very top of the garland.

As the lid of the sewing box was lifted, the children watched in breathless silence. And when Miss Holmes lifted the Lady up they gave a little sigh of satisfaction to see how lovely she was.

"Now then," said Miss Holmes, "I'm going to inspect the garland one last time to make sure it's ready, before we put the Lady in her place. I shall lay her here" – she laid the Lady on top of her desk – "and no one –" she glanced round sternly – "I say *no one* is to touch her."

They nodded solemnly. And then *nearly* everyone followed Miss Holmes out into the porch, where the finished garland stood.

Someone had stayed behind in the classroom. For as they stood round admiring the garland there was a terrific crash. Followed by a terrible hush.

"Oh!" cried Miss Holmes, putting her hand to her cheek and closing her eyes for a moment. "Surely it can't be . . ."

But it was. The children parted to let her run through into the school room, and then followed.

There stood Edmund, head hanging and cheeks like tomatoes. And there, at his feet, lay the Lady. Her smooth, flat, yellow hair was dishevelled at the back, but she lay face down, so the children couldn't see the front of her.

Miss Holmes said: "Edmund! How *could* you?" in a voice that was more unhappy than cross.

"I only wanted to look," muttered Edmund, feeling everyone's furious gaze upon him.

Miss Holmes picked up the Lady, and turned her over. They all gasped in dismay. There was a big jagged hole in the middle of her smooth china face, where her nose should have been. Her shiny blue eyes still stared peacefully at the world, but she no longer looked beautiful. "Oh dear, oh dear," said Miss

Holmes, turning the Lady this way and that in her hands. "Oh dear, oh dear, oh dear. . . ." She didn't seem able to collect her thoughts at all, poor woman, and who could blame her?

"Edmund, how could you *do* such a thing?" asked Laura in a ferocious whisper. She had never felt so mortified and ashamed.

"Because he's a horrid little beast, that's why!" shouted Ella May, unable to contain herself a second longer. "He's ruined everything!" And she hurled her crown to the ground and burst into tears.

"Shush, Ella May," said Miss Holmes, looking distracted. "We must think of something. We can't possibly abandon the procession."

Laura's brain raced. She was overcome with shame, that her brother had done such an awful thing and spoiled what had been a lovely day. Then all at once she remembered something.

"Please, ma'am." she cried, standing on tiptoe and waving her hand in the air to catch Miss Holmes's eye amid the confusion. "Please, ma'am, we've got a doll you could use!"

"What's that, Laura?" said Miss Holmes, flapping her hands at the others to make them be quiet. "You have a doll?"

All the children, and especially the girls, turned and gawped at Laura in disbelief. They all knew that the Lady had to be a proper china doll, elegantly dressed, and no one had a doll like that at home.

Laura continued bravely: "We had a cupboard full of old lumber. When Mrs Herring came to sort it out, there was a china doll in it. And she gave her to me."

Miss Holmes heaved a sigh of relief.

"She sounds perfect, Laura. Do you think you could bring her tomorrow?"

Laura's brain raced again. She was willing Edmund not to say anything silly. The doll Mrs Herring had left behind had once been a good doll. But after years with the old lumber she was filthy, and her clothes were in rags, and her hair was all matted and tangled. Laura took a deep breath. "Yes," she said. "I'll bring her."

On the way home Edmund said to Laura: "But what are you going to *do*?" To which Laura replied: "Mother will help us."

When they got back they told their mother the whole sad story. She listened with a serious face, but when they'd finished she smiled.

"Very well! I'll make your lady look pretty. Come, let's see what we can do."

After that it became an exciting evening, as they set to work on the bedraggled old doll. When their mother had pushed a bit more stuffing into her cloth body and stitched up the holes, Edmund gave her china face a good wash, and combed her tangled hair.

Laura made a petticoat for the Lady out of two white handkerchiefs, because her sewing wasn't all that good. They couldn't find any blue stuff for her dress, but they did have some pretty green and pink snippets left over from Laura's bedroom curtains, and some bits of white cotton lace from an old hat. From these, the children's mother made a lovely dress with a lace trim and a green sash, and even a little bonnet to match with a ribbon that tied under the chin.

It was quite late when they finished, and the old doll was transformed. She actually seemed to be smiling more, as if she knew how nice she looked. When

Laura's father came in from inspecting the Dinner Pig, he said: "Well I never. She's a real picture." And he put his hand down for a moment on Laura's mother's shoulder.

It was the same the next day. Everyone was absolutely delighted with the new Lady, and they all agreed that if anything she was even more beautiful than the first one.

She was set on top of the garland, with all the flowers round her, and Laura was so proud she thought she might burst. In honour of all her hard work, and of having saved the day, Laura was given the job of carrying the money box, at the very front of the procession. She no longer minded in the least about Ella May being Queen. She didn't think it was possible to be any happier. She was even quite grateful to Edmund for having broken the Lady in the first place.

Round the rise they went, to every door, with Laura leading the way, and the green and pink and white Lady bobbing and nodding on her seat of flowers.

At the door of the end house Laura
knocked, and her mother answered.

"Ah, the May Day procession," she
said. "And doesn't it look lovely?" And
she fetched a coin and put it in the box,
all very proper. But as she closed the
door Laura caught her eye. And it
definitely winked.